SNOT
STEW

SNOT STEW

Bill Wallace

drawings by LISA McCUE

HOLIDAY HOUSE / NEW YORK

Library of Congress Cataloging-in-Publication Data

Wallace, Bill
Snot stew.

Summary: Brother and sister cats are taken in by a
family and learn the pleasures and dangers of living
alongside humans.
[1. Cats—Fiction. 2. Brothers and sisters—Fiction]
I. Title.
PZ7.W15473Sn 1989   [Fic]   88-31976
ISBN 0-8234-0745-4

To NIKKI and JUSTIN—who still like to play

SNOT
STEW

Chapter 1

Our mama was the best mama in the whole wide world. She did all sorts of stuff for us. She gave us milk so we would grow up to be big and strong. And she gave us baths with her tongue, which was dry and rough, but it felt good anyway.

When we got older, she quit giving us milk and caught mice for us. Mice are about the yummiest thing in the whole world! They're made up of all sorts of good healthy things, like meat and bones with lots of fiber, vitamins, and minerals. They taste real good, and they're fun to play with, too.

"Don't play with your food," Mama always said. "Unless it's a mouse. Then it's okay."

She'd bring the mice back to our house—a soft pile of hay in a big wooden box in the barn. Mama

3

said it was an old icebox. Usually, cats don't live in iceboxes, but this one had been left in the Burkes' barn for so long that a hole had rotted in the side. We used the hole as our door. And nobody ever moved the icebox, so it was the perfect place for a home.

"Besides," Mama said, "it's warm in the winter and cool in the summer."

Mama made us watch while she gave herself a bath. She said that we would need to learn how to take a bath by ourselves before too long. We didn't know what she meant, not until the day she came home and told us she was leaving.

We all laughed and climbed over each other and tumbled and swatted as we rushed to greet her at the door to get the mouse she brought.

Only, this time there was no mouse.

"I'm leaving," Mama said flatly.

We laughed again. Chris jumped on Mama's back so she would play with him. But she didn't play. She swatted him real hard and knocked him rolling against the side of our house.

"I'll be away for a few days, and when I come back, you must be gone."

"But why, Mama?" we all meowed at once. "This is our home."

"This is *my* home," Mama answered. "I'm going

to have another family, and I need my home for raising my babies. You're old enough and big enough to be out on your own."

"But Mama . . ." we moaned.

"I've taught you how to catch mice. I've taught you how to take a bath. I've warned you about people and how you can't trust them and how it's best to stay away from them. I've told you about Butch, the Burkes' dog, and how mean and nasty he is and how he would just love to eat a soft, juicy kitten. I've taught you all that I can. It's time for you to grow up and leave home."

Then she turned and squeezed out the door.

We all meowed and begged her to come back. She didn't.

After a while we talked it over and decided that Mama was only teasing and that she really would come back—because she had always taken care of us.

The next morning Mama wasn't back.

We meowed louder that day, meowed and meowed and meowed. Only, Mama never came with our mouse. She never came to give us a bath.

"I've had it," Chris meowed on the second morning Mama was gone. He swished his tail in big circles as he looked out the hole in the side of our icebox. "I'm hungry. I can catch my own mouse." Then he left.

That afternoon Tiffany left, too. She wasn't as sure of herself as Chris. But she was just as hungry. Then Jeff left that night, and so did Lisa.

Toby and I were the only ones who stayed. We cried and meowed all night. The next morning we cried and meowed even more. I don't ever remember being so hungry or so lonely.

"I guess Mama really *isn't* coming back," I told Toby.

He buried his face in his paws.

"No, she isn't," he finally meowed.

He had such a sad look on his face I could hardly stand it. So I jumped on his back, hoping that a little romp would make him feel better. Only, Toby didn't want to play. He just lay there and let me bite his ears.

"What are we going to do, Kikki?" he moaned.

I lay down beside him. I swished my tail against his ear.

"I guess we have to grow up," I meowed. "I guess we have to leave home—or we'll starve."

We cried and meowed some more. But before we could leave, a terrible thing happened.

Our house began to rock. It creaked and moaned. The walls lifted on one side, then the other.

All at once the whole side of our house was gone. Light flooded in. Toby and I froze. We huddled together, pressing ourselves as hard as we could against each other for safety.

There was a loud *boom.* Our house fell over, and we were left out in the open, on the floor of the big barn.

Chapter 2

A cloud of dust belched up from the hay. I peeked out from under Toby's ear, where I was trying to hide. I blinked, trying to clear the dust from my eyes.

A people stood there. It was a man people. He towered above us. He glared down with a mean and nasty look. I was scared and wanted to run. Only, I couldn't. Toby couldn't either.

I tried to get to my feet. But I was shaking so hard nothing would move.

The man people frowned. He scratched his chin with his huge paw.

"I'll be," his deep, roaring voice boomed. "That much racket, I thought there must be fifty cats under here. Not just two."

Then he leaned down. His huge paw reached out and snatched Toby up by the back of the neck. I closed my eyes. I was trembling so hard I thought I was going to get buried in the hay.

Then his other big paw grabbed me. He lifted me from my bed where my house used to be. I felt everything go stiff. My arms went out straight. My feet tried to run, but the ground wasn't there. There was nothing but air.

I twisted and turned and wiggled. I felt my claws pop out. And I cried and cried.

Suddenly, I was looking the man people square in the eye. He held me by the back of the neck.

"You're a feisty little thing." His voice was a roar.

It made my ears lie back flat against my neck. I was so scared I wanted to die. I twisted and flopped some more. It didn't do any good.

"Oh, Daddy," another people squealed. "A kitten. Oh, Daddy, may I see?"

"Me too, Daddy. I want to see one, too."

It was yet another people. There were people things all over the place. Loud, noisy, scary people things. Everywhere!

I stuck my claws out again and was so stiff I thought I was going to break.

I scrunched my eyes tight and glared at the man people with the meanest look I had.

If I could just get my claws into you, I thought. Just one time. I bet you'd let me go then.

The man people only smiled. Another man people rushed up beside him. It was a boy I think. He was smaller than the man. He had blue cloth on his bottom half and red checked cloth on his top half, and his hair was brown—the same brown as the spot next to Toby's tail.

"Let me see, Daddy," he squealed. "May I hold him? Please. Please. Please!"

The man people handed Toby to the boy. I shuddered again.

Were they going to eat him? Were the people things going to bite my brother's head off? Were they going to toss him in the air and hold him by the tail and then gobble him down—like we did a mouse?

I couldn't stand to watch. I closed my eyes.

"Meeeeooooowww," I called, which meant "You're my brother, Toby. I love you. Good-bye!"

The boy people didn't toss him in the air. He didn't hold him by the tail. He didn't bite him. He just cuddled Toby in his arms. He held him tight and stroked his fur and talked real soft in his ear.

Another voice behind me made me jump. I stuck out my claws again.

"Oh, Daddy," it squeaked. "May I have that one?

Please, Daddy. She's so cute. May I, Daddy? Please, oh please. Please. Please."

My eyes flashed open. I saw another people right beside me. This people thing was different from the other two. It had on a cloth thing that was the same color from its top to its bottom. It was blue and full and rustled in the breeze. Its hair was long and yellow-colored, like the spot near Toby's ears. Its voice was higher and not so loud. It must be a girl people.

"I don't know," the man people growled in my ear. "This one's not as gentle as that other one. I'm afraid this one's scared."

"Darned right I'm scared," I meowed at him. "Just let me get my claws into you, and I'll show you how scared . . ."

"Tell you what," the man people said. "Let's let this one go. You and Ben can play with the other one."

"But Daddy," the girl people whined. "Ben's got a kitty. I want a kitty, too. Please, Daddy. Ben never shares anything with me. I want my own kitty."

The man people squeezed harder on the back of my neck. I felt him shake.

"Now hold on just a minute." His voice was deeper. "I never said anything about keeping them.

I thought you could just play with them out here
. . . and . . . and . . . Ben! Where are you going
with that cat?"

Toby and the boy people who was holding him
disappeared out the door. The man followed him,
still holding onto my neck.

"Ben. Come back here with that cat. Ben, mind
me! Ben!"

Ben just kept going. The girl people was right
beside me.

"Daddy. Please. Please. May I have one, too?"
She was jumping up and down, grabbing at me.
The man lifted me higher. My tail twisted, but all I
could do was flip and flop in midair.

"Daddy, it's such a pretty kitty. Please, Daddy.
Oh, please . . ."

"Now, Sarah . . ."

She jumped up and down again.

"Oh, please . . . please . . . please . . ."

Toby and the boy people named Ben disappeared
through a big door in the other barn. I just knew I'd
never see my brother again.

"Daddy. Please. Pretty please with sugar on it.
Please!"

The man people named Daddy sighed. He turned
around to look at the girl people named Sarah.

"Oh, all right. I don't much take to cats in the

house. They need to be out here in the barn to get rid of the mice. But if you really want her . . ."

"Oh, Daddy," the Sarah people squealed as she jumped up and down. "I do, I do, I do."

Daddy handed me to Sarah. He put her paw where his had been at the loose skin on the back of my neck.

"You be careful," he warned. "She's scared and she'll scratch you. Don't let her get her claws . . . Sarah, don't let her get near your eyes . . . Sarah . . ."

The girl people wasn't listening to Daddy. She took off running across the big yard, with me dangling in the air. She ran across the big open, outdoor space between the barns.

This is it, I told myself with a loud meow. This is the end of me. They're going to take me into that other barn and eat me.

Chapter 3

The people things *didn't* eat me.

When we got to the other barn, Sarah put me down on the ground. She held me by the back of the neck and patted me and talked—real, real soft.

I liked the sound of her soft talk. It was much nicer, much more pleasant than the whining I had heard earlier.

And finally, she let me go.

Now was my chance. Freedom at last. I took off. Only, the floor under my feet was slick as could be. I ran and my feet just spun. I ran harder. My feet just spun more. Finally, they took hold of the slickery floor. I went flying and ran as hard as I could.

There was an opening in front of me. But the floor

was so slick, when I tried to turn, I couldn't. I went crashing into the wall. I hit it so hard I almost knocked myself out. Still, I kept running.

Now I was in a different part of the barn, where the floor was soft and felt good under my feet. I could really hold on and move here.

I ran and ran and ran, trying to find a way out of this barn so I could get back to my own barn. Only, there was no way out. This barn was closed tight. Finally, I found a place to hide. It was under a big long thing with soft pillowy things on it. Its bottom was close to the ground, and it was dark under there. I sat, trembling and panting and shaking.

I was breathing so hard I could barely hear. But above my panting I heard another people voice in the other room.

"Leave her be, Sarah," the voice said. It was a soft voice, a voice that sounded gentle, almost nice. "She's scared. Just let her explore her new home for a while. Let her relax some."

"I want to play with her, Mother," I heard Sarah whine again.

"There's plenty of time for that," the mother voice answered. "Just leave her be for a little while."

Nobody came after me. I was alone under the long dark thing with the pillowy things. After a

while I started feeling a little safer. I licked my paws and cleaned my face and looked around.

This barn wasn't like the barn where my house was. It was brighter, and there were more colors and things to look at.

First off, there was no hay on the floor. It was covered with this soft, fluffy cloth. It felt good to dig my claws in it and sharpen them. There were things all around—little things on the walls, big things like the thing I was hiding under, and things with short legs. There were things with long legs and flat wood tops on them, too.

Suddenly, two big blue eyes were staring at me.

"Mother," Sarah called. "She's under the couch."

I felt myself jump. I scooted back, farther into the safety of my dark place called The Couch.

"Leave her alone," the Mother people called.

Sarah went and sat on one of the other things that looked like The Couch, only it was smaller.

"May I sit in the chair and wait for her to come out, Mother?"

"No, Sarah. I'm making some stew for supper. Why don't you come in the kitchen and help me?"

Sarah left.

I felt my tail, which was big and all fuzzed up, start to relax. The fur went down. I was safe again. At least for a while.

But what about Toby? I wondered. Would I ever see him again? Was he lost, forever? My poor, poor Toby.

I meowed his name over and over and over.

Chapter 4

It seemed like forever, but finally, Toby heard my cries.

"I'm here," he meowed.

"Where?" My ears perked up. I crawled to the edge of my hiding place under The Couch, so I could see better.

"Right here," he meowed.

Toby came walking across the floor. He really wasn't walking. It was more like a strut. He ambled around, swishing his tail from side to side. He had a real "big shot" look on his face.

"Under here, quick," I meowed. "It's safe under The Couch."

Toby didn't seem interested in hiding though. He

strutted across the room. He climbed right up in The Chair, where Sarah had sat, and started licking his paws.

"Toby. Down here. Quick," I called.

He just raised his eyebrows and moved his head to the side, like he was about to go to sleep.

"What are you hiding under there for?" he said, real cocky-like. "It's much softer up here in this The Chair than it is under there, The Couch. Come on up."

I felt my eyes get wide.

"Oh no, I can't. They'll get me. They'll . . . they'll . . ."

Toby sneered.

"Oh, quit being such a baby, Kikki. They're not going to get you. People things are nice."

I shook my head.

"Oh, Toby. Are you nuts? Mama told us you couldn't trust people things. She said they could be mean sometimes. Remember her telling about her friend who got caught by people things, and they tied a tin can to his tail? And about a tom cat she used to know—people tried to shoot him just because he was singing to Mama."

Toby licked his paws and shrugged.

"Well, maybe some people things are mean. But the Burkes aren't. They're nice!"

"Nice?" I stuck my head farther out from under The Couch.

Toby nodded.

"Real nice. My boy people's name is Ben. He pets me and rubs my back. He even scratched me behind my ears." His eyes kind of got that dreamy look in them. "It felt *good*."

"Really?"

Toby smiled and licked his other paw.

"Really. The girl people is called Sarah. She petted me too. She pet softer than Ben, but it felt okay. The big man people is named Daddy, and the other girl people . . . well, they call her Mother, I think. They're all nice. They even fed me."

My eyes got big. I was far enough out from under The Couch that I could raise my front end up.

"Food?"

Suddenly, I realized how far from my safe hiding place I had crawled. I jerked and looked around quickly in all directions. There was nobody there, no people things trying to sneak up on me.

"Food?" I asked again.

Toby smoothed his whiskers down with his paws.

"That's right. Milk, even."

"MILK!"

I was clear out from under The Couch. I walked over to The Chair. I put my paws up on it, where

Toby was sitting. I looked him straight in the eye.

"Real milk? Like Mama's?"

Toby quit smoothing down his long whiskers.

"Well, not quite like Mama's. It tasted different. And it was cold instead of warm. But it was sure *gooood!*"

He rolled over on his back and stuck his paws straight up in the air. I could see how round his tummy looked.

"Real honest-to-goodness milk?"

"That's right," Toby yawned.

I climbed up on The Chair so I could look him in the eye again.

"I'm starving," I meowed. "How can I get some?"

Toby rolled over on his side and curled his paws under his chest.

"Simple. All you've got to do is go in there. They call it The Kitchen. It's in a saucer, on the floor."

I frowned.

"That's all? Just walk in there and get it? And that's all there is to it?"

Toby yawned again.

"Well . . . no. You might have to get petted or get your ears scratched. But that isn't bad, either. Fact is, it felt pretty good."

I shuddered.

"Oh no. I couldn't do that. I couldn't let those people things get hold of me. I . . . I . . ."

There was a noise from the other room—a loud clanging sound.

Instantly, my tail shot straight up. I jumped in the air and spun around. I made a mad dash for my safe place under The Couch.

From there, I could see into The Kitchen. The girl people called Mother was picking a pan up off the floor. She wiped it with a cloth and put it back from where it had fallen. She picked another thing up out of some water and wiped it with a towel, too. As she wiped, she hummed to herself. It was a soft, pretty sound, a sound that flowed through the barn. It was deeper but not as clear as the sound the birds made in our barn.

I relaxed again and felt my tail unfuzz. Maybe Toby was right. Maybe these Burke people weren't the bad people things Mama had warned us about.

Still, I had to be careful. I had to stay here where it was safe. But . . . but . . .

Milk?

That sure sounded good.

Chapter 5

Mother put some round things on a big thing with long legs and a flat top. They made a kind of *tink* sound when she put them down.

My nose kept twitching. There was a beautiful smell in the air. It made my nose wiggle and my mouth feel wet and drippy inside.

I didn't know what the smell was, but it was certainly WONDERFUL.

Then Mother yelled, "Supper. Everybody come and eat."

She closed a big wood thing that stood between where we were and The Kitchen. It kept us from seeing what was happening.

Toby had noticed the wonderful smell, too. He just got to the wood thing when Mother closed it.

He stuck his nose down at the crack underneath the wood thing and sniffed.

"Meow." He told me it sure smelled good. "Meow." Real good!

I felt safer with the wood thing there—with the people in the other room of the barn and me and Toby in here. I crawled out from under The Couch.

We could hear tinking and clanging and pattering from the other room. Mother and Daddy and Ben and Sarah talked and tinked and clattered for a long, long while. Then everyone got sort of quiet. All at once the wood thing by Toby and me opened.

I jumped back. My tail fuzzed up. Toby didn't move. He stood there, looking into The Kitchen.

I let my tail drop and moved up beside my brother.

"You two ready for supper?" Mother asked. "Come on in. It's all fixed."

Toby walked past her. He got real close and leaned against her leg. Mother didn't kick him or try to bite him or anything. She just stood there and let him rub.

"Come on," Toby meowed. "Let's see what smells so good."

Cautiously, one step at a time, I followed him. Mother scraped some food onto the round things that went *tink* on the table. She put one bowl down

in front of Toby. She scraped some more into a
second bowl and put that down next to me.

"Stew," Mother announced. "You two hungry for
stew?"

Toby went straight to his bowl. He stuck in his
head and started eating. Carefully, I eased up
beside him.

This Stew stuff smells marvelous, I thought. But
what if . . .

I jumped back.

"Go on," Mother coaxed in a soft voice. "I know
you're hungry. Go on, little girl. Nobody's going to
hurt you."

Her voice was very gentle and friendly. I moved
back to the bowl. I kind of snuck up on it—step by
careful step.

I was scared. But mostly, I was *hungry*. And this
Stew smelled so . . . so . . .

I took a bite.

It was delicious. It was the best stuff I ever
tasted. I LOVED IT!

Stew was better than milk. It was even better
than mice. It had orange things and yellow things
and a few green things in it, all mixed up with gravy
and lots and lots of meat.

And I was *soooooo* hungry.

I ate and ate. I didn't even notice when Mother

knelt down beside me and started petting me. I didn't mind though. It didn't feel bad. Besides, it felt so good to have something to eat.

In a little while she left, and Sarah came. She sat down beside me and crossed her legs. She started stroking the hair on my back. She even scratched behind my ears.

Toby was right. That did kind of feel good.

It felt *great* to have my tummy full. I guess I hadn't ever been so hungry before. Of course, I hadn't had a thing to eat since my mama left. Nothing at all. But Stew was fabulous.

Sarah put a hand under my tummy when I finished eating. For a second I thought she was going to pick me up. She didn't though. I was glad that she didn't because, as full as my tummy was, that would have hurt.

Instead, she stroked my fur some more and scratched my ears. Then she left for a place called Bed. Mother told her she had to.

I licked every bit of the Stew from my bowl, and when I was finished, I went back and crawled under The Couch.

"Maybe people things aren't so bad after all," I thought as I licked my paws and washed my whiskers. Even the Stew that was stuck to my whiskers tasted good.

Toby curled up in The Chair and went to sleep. I finished my bath. Ben had to go to Bed, too. Mother and Daddy stayed up and listened to a thing called The Stereo. I liked the sound that came from it. It was almost as good as the humming I had heard Mother do when she was working in The Kitchen.

I closed my eyes.

People were okay. At least, the Burkes were. They were nice. Besides that, Mother made terrific Stew.

Chapter 6

I learned a lot during the next few days. I learned that the barn where the Burke family lived was called a house. My safe place was called the couch—instead of The Couch. The round things with long legs were tables, and there were lamps on them, where light came from.

The Burkes had names for the different rooms in the house, too. My couch was in the living room. They had bedrooms for sleeping, a playroom for watching a machine called a TV, and the kitchen.

The kitchen was my favorite place. That's where Mother or Sarah fed me.

They had some dry, crunchy stuff that they called cat food. I didn't much care for that. Once a day Sarah would open a can of "real" cat food. It tasted

like meat. She would give me some in my bowl. It
was good, but not nearly as good as Stew.

Things went pretty well in the Burkes' house. I
liked my girl named Sarah. She was mine because I
was hers. She would call me Her Cat. She would
pet me and scratch me behind my ears. She talked
to me real softly and was never mean to me. It made
me purr and feel warm and toasty inside.

Toby belonged to the boy named Ben. He and
Toby liked to play. Ben would drag a string across
the floor. Toby would pretend it was a mouse and
sneak up, then pounce on it. Ben would laugh and
grab Toby and playfully rub his fur the wrong way.
Toby would arch his back way up, like he was really
mad. He'd kind of pounce, sideways, like he was
going to get Ben. They would roughhouse and play
for hours and hours.

Besides getting petted and rubbed and fed cat
food and watching Toby and his boy play rough boy
games, I learned that there were some Rules around
the place.

Mother didn't like us to climb up on her table in
the kitchen to look at the plates. (I guess she didn't
want anybody looking at her plates except people
things.) If we did, she would yell at us and swat at
us with her dish towel.

Daddy didn't like us to sharpen our claws on the couch or chair or rug. (But where's a cat supposed to sharpen his claws if not on stuff like that?) Anyway, if we did, he would yell at us in his loudest, deepest voice. Once he even swatted Toby with a newspaper. That scared me so much I hid in my safe place under the couch for one whole night.

There were also some things on shelves in the living room that Mother called Trinkets. There were glass birds and statues of people dancing and a pink glass bowl. It had flowers and stems carved into the side of the glass.

One day Mother found us up there. We were just looking. But she started yelling and screaming and calling us all sorts of bad names. I took off for my safe place. She chased Toby all around the living room, until he finally ran under the couch where I was.

He was all puffed up and breathing hard. Only he didn't want me to know how scared he had been.

"She isn't so tough," he said, slicking his fur down with his rough tongue. "She isn't so tough. I'll show her."

Toby did show her, too. The very next morning, he climbed back up on the shelves and started prowling around. Toby's being up there must have startled one

of Mother's birds, because it flew off the shelf. The dumb thing couldn't fly though, since it was made out of glass. So all it did was fall on the floor.

There was a loud *CRASH-tinkle*.

Toby stood real still. I ran for the safe place.

Then . . .

Mother came in. She knelt down and looked at her poor dead bird. Her bottom lip quivered as she glared up at Toby. Before he could move, she grabbed him.

"Meooowww," he cried.

All of a sudden Mother came after me. Why, I don't know. I hadn't done anything. I'd been under the couch all the time.

But she reached under anyway and grabbed me. She didn't have a good hold, so I started to crawl away. Her fingers slipped, but she caught my tail and held it firmly. She started pulling. I dug my claws into the carpet.

It was no use. She just pulled harder. I couldn't hang on.

"Why me?" I meowed. "Why me?"

Mother didn't pay any attention. Once I was out from under the couch, she grabbed me by the back of the neck. She held Toby and me both at arm's length, took us to the back door, and threw us out.

My legs went stiff. I twisted and turned and used

my tail to straighten me out. And like a good cat I landed on my feet.

Toby landed next to me. He was all fuzzed up and looked rather indignant about the whole thing. The fur behind his neck was ruffled, so he gave a shake of his head.

"How dare you throw me out like some scrap of garbage," he growled, "I'll show you. I'll . . ."

I marched right over to Toby and swatted him across the head with my paw.

"You won't show her anything," I growled. "This is all your fault. You stay off that shelf. If she ever lets us back in the barn—I mean house—you stay away from Mother's trinkets."

Toby just ruffled his fur and strutted off.

I arched my back way up. "I mean it, Toby. You understand?"

He flipped his tail.

"Well . . . while we're out here," he called over his shoulder, "let's go explore."

I was a little frightened of the outdoors, but I followed Toby. There were all sorts of neat things to see. There was a big oak tree by the back door. There were bushes to prowl around and rub my back on. There was dirt to roll in. There was even grass. I nibbled some of it. It didn't taste good, but it felt good on my tummy.

Then Toby found the hole under the wood fence.

"Come on," he called, sticking his head through the hole. "I bet there's a whole new world out there. Let's go explore it, too."

"Wait, Toby," I meowed back. "Don't you think we should make sure there aren't any bad things out there first?"

But Toby didn't listen. His tail disappeared through the crack in the fence.

I poked my whiskers into the hole. They didn't even touch, so I knew it was plenty big enough to get through. Still, all I did was stick my head out the other side. I wanted to look this new world over.

Finally, I went to join Toby. This new world didn't look bad at all. It was much, much, much bigger than the world in the house. And it was much, much, much bigger than the world in the backyard. Everything was open and wide and free.

Surely nothing bad could live in this world, I told myself.

The only trouble was, something bad *did* live here.

Butch!

Chapter 7

The new world—the outside, outside world—was marvelous. It was big. I could see for a long, long way. There was another fence, but it was made with wire—instead of wood, like the fence we'd just crawled through.

There were big animals behind the fence. I mean BIG!

They had long tails and short horns and were white with big black spots. They said: "Moo."

"Moo" didn't make any sense, so I didn't bother to walk out and talk to them.

There was a small fenced-in place over to the side. That fence was different still. It was made with wire too, but the wire was small and twisted into little square-like things. I guess the wire was smaller because the animals who lived there were smaller. They looked a little like the birds on Mother's trinket shelf. Only they weren't made out of glass. They walked around and bit at stuff on the ground with their long, sharp mouths. They said: "Cluck, cluck."

I felt my mouth twitch up on one side. Hmmm, I thought, outside animals are hard to understand.

Then, all of a sudden, I heard another sound. It was a loud "BOW-WOW!"

Toby and I both jumped. We looked beside the fence, where the sound had come from. Down at the end some huge monster glared at us around the corner. His eyes were brown and round. His face was black as the night. His lips curled, and I could see white fangs, glistening beneath his pink gums.

Toby and I froze. I trembled, watching the monster.

Suddenly, his "bow-wow" became a loud growl. He charged around the corner of the fence. He was racing straight toward us.

My tail puffed up, nearly as big around as I was. My claws came out. I scampered back through the hole. I ran straight to the tree and raced up it. (I'd never climbed a tree before. I don't know how I did it, but when I looked around, there I was—perched up in the branches.)

"Toby," I meowed. "Toby. Run. Run!"

The loud "bow-wow" came again. Toby scooted through the hole in the fence below me. His tail was fuzzed up, just as big around as mine was. Instead of running for the tree like I did, Toby stopped and looked back toward the fence.

There was nothing there. No sound. No monster.

Then a black snout appeared, with white teeth. It roared. The teeth snapped shut—over and over again as it roared.

Toby jumped back. He started for the tree. But just before he got there, he stopped.

"Hurry, Toby," I called. "Up here, where it's safe."

Toby stood, watching the hole. After a little while the snout and the white fangs disappeared. Toby started back toward the fence.

"No, Toby," I meowed. "It'll get you! Up here, quick!"

Toby just ignored me. He stood a little way back from the hole. He leaned down, looking. Then he moved closer.

I shut my eyes.

"Watch this," he called.

I forced my eyes to open, but only a crack.

He started prancing back and forth in front of the hole. He strolled, casually, one way and then the other. Each time he walked past the hole, he got closer.

Suddenly, there was another roar. The black snout stuck through the hole again. The white fangs snapped.

Toby froze, but he didn't run. I couldn't watch. But the growling and snapping stopped. I peeked.

Toby was looking up at me. He had the biggest smile I ever saw on his face.

"The monster's too fat to get through the hole," he meowed. "He's too big to fit. All he can do is growl and snap. But he can't touch me. Ha Ha!"

Toby began strutting back and forth in front of the hole again.

> "Fatty, fatty two-by-four,
> Couldn't get through
> The bathroom door.
> So he did it
> On the floor."

Toby chanted over and over.

Finally, the monster stuck his snout through the hole and growled and snapped some more.

Toby just laughed. "This is fun," he called. "Come on."

I shook my head.

"What if . . ."

Toby just flipped his tail. "What if, nothing," he

cut me off. "He's too big. He can't get through. Come on."

As carefully and slowly as could be, I eased down the tree. I walked just a little way and stopped. Tilting my head to the side, I tried to look through the crack to see if the monster was still there.

"What is it, Toby?" I asked, leaning my head the other way.

"It's Butch," Toby meowed.

"Butch? What's a Butch?"

Toby flipped his tail.

"Mother told us about him, remember? Butch is the Burkes' dog. She said he was black as night and had long, white fangs and roared instead of talked. She said he would just love to eat a soft, juicy kitten. Remember?"

I felt the hair on my back tingle.

"I remember."

Toby started prancing back and forth again, chanting "Fatty, fatty . . ." Only nothing happened.

He looked at me. Then, frowning, he looked back at the hole.

"Fat Butch must have gone," Toby complained. "I better have a look."

"No. *No!*" I cried. "Don't stick your head through there. If he's hiding beside the fence, he'll bite it off."

Toby frowned.

"You may be right." He sat down beside the hole and looked around. "Ah! There's a way I can find out."

I noticed him looking up at the top of the fence. There was a board that ran just beneath the top. Toby looked around a while longer. Then, quicker than I could blink, he jumped up on the picnic table and on up to that wood rail.

"Careful, Toby. Don't fall."

The wood was not very wide. Toby walked along it, just like he was on the ground. He was such a good fence walker he didn't even have to be careful. The wood rail was so close to the top of the fence Toby didn't even have to stretch to look over.

"He's not down there," Toby meowed.

He sounded almost sad about it.

"Good," I called. "Now, get down before you fall. Let's go back to the door. Maybe Mother will let us in."

Toby just flipped his tail.

"No. I want to find out where Butch went. Teasing him is fun. I want to do it some more."

Toby walked the rail all the way to the corner of the fence. He turned and kept going. About halfway down the other side he stopped.

I watched him for a long time. He would peek

over the fence, then look back across the yard at the hole, then peek over the fence again.

My whiskers wiggled, wondering what he was up to.

Suddenly, Toby jumped over the fence! My eyes popped open so wide I thought they were going to bust out of my head.

I heard Butch bark. I shuddered. The sound of his roar raced toward the corner of the fence, then down the long straight part, toward the hole.

The monster had eaten my Toby. My brother was a goner.

There was a flash. Toby shot through the hole in the fence. Right behind him, the black snout and the snapping white fangs appeared.

I jumped. Toby turned and leaned down so he could see through the hole.

> "Fatty, fatty. Two-by-four
> Couldn't get through
> The bathroom door.
> So he did it
> On the floor."

Toby giggled over and over as he strutted and flipped his tail.

"Toby, please come away from there. That Butch is going to eat you. Please."

Toby just strutted and chanted more.

After a while Butch went away, and Toby jumped back up on the fence rail.

"Toby," I warned. "Don't. You keep messin' with that dog, he's gonna get you."

Toby just flipped his tail and laughed.

"He's fat and he's slow, too," Toby sneered. "He can't get me. I'm the world's fastest cat. And he's the world's slowest, fattest dog."

Then Toby jumped over the fence again.

I hated this game. I hated Toby teasing the monster Butch like this. I just knew something bad was going to happen. I just knew Butch was going to catch Toby.

But again and again Toby and Butch played their game. And every time, Toby managed to squeeze through the hole in the fence, just ahead of those snapping white fangs.

I guess Toby would have gone on playing his game and teasing Butch forever if it hadn't been for Mother.

Toby had just jumped on the picnic table and then onto the wood rail when Mother opened the back door. She got her voice up real high and called: "Here kitty, kitty, kitty."

My ears perked up. She held the door open with her foot. There were two bowls in her hands.

"Come on, Kitty. You want some stew?"

I felt my ears perk straight up.

Stew?

Toby jumped down from the fence and bounded across the yard toward her. I raced after him.

I hated the game Toby was playing. But . . .

I LOVE STEW!!!

Chapter 8

The next day, and from that day on, Mother would let us out in the backyard. It was much nicer to be let out than to be thrown out.

After a few days I liked going outside. I liked the way the sunshine felt warm on my fur. I liked the way the grass smelled and the way the bushes scratched my back. I liked to roll in the dirt and then stand up and shake and watch the little puffs and clouds of dust drift all around me. I liked to listen to the birds and sometimes try to sneak up and catch one—only I never did.

I liked almost everything outdoors—everything except Butch and the dumb game Toby played with him.

There were other dumb games around the Burkes' house. Like the "Name the Cat" game.

Ben and Sarah and Mother and Daddy decided they were going to give Toby and me names. They sat down at the kitchen table one night and thought of all the different names they could. Then they voted on the ones they liked.

They decided that they would name Toby Rambo. Now that was a dumb name if I ever heard one.

They decided to name me Tic-tac. That name was even worse.

Toby and I decided if they were going to play "Name the Cat," then we were going to play "Ignore the People."

Whenever they called us by our made-up names, we wouldn't come. I learned to flip my tail, just like Toby did, and we'd walk away from them. If we were sleeping or catnapping, we wouldn't even look up.

The only time we *did* answer to our people names was when it was time to eat. When there was food, it didn't matter what they called us, just so long as we got fed!

There was another game Ben and Sarah played. Toby and I called it "Pushie-Shove" or "The Hit Game." Ben and Sarah played that game with their toys.

Sarah would grab one of Ben's trucks and try to run away with it. Ben would hold onto it. Then they would push and shove and push and shove and pull and yank.

Other times Ben would try to grab Sarah's doll. She would chase him through the house, yelling: "Mine, *mine!*" If she caught him, she'd hit him. Then he'd hit her back. Then she'd run to Mother and cry: "Mama, Mama. Ben hit me."

And Ben would cry: "She hit me first."

And Sarah would whine: "But he stole my doll."

And Mother would say: "Quit fussing or I'll send you to your room."

So Ben and Sarah would go off, wait a while, then start the game again.

Toby and I learned to play some games, too. Our favorite was "People Scratch." We learned if we climbed up in Mother's lap while she was reading, she would rub us and scratch us behind the ears. Sarah would play the game, too. But sometimes I had to rub against her and meow so she would notice. Daddy didn't always play right. Sometimes when we would jump in his lap, he would pet us. Other times he would shove us off on the floor and growl at us. It was hard to tell which he'd do.

People Scratch was a nice game, though. Toby and I liked it.

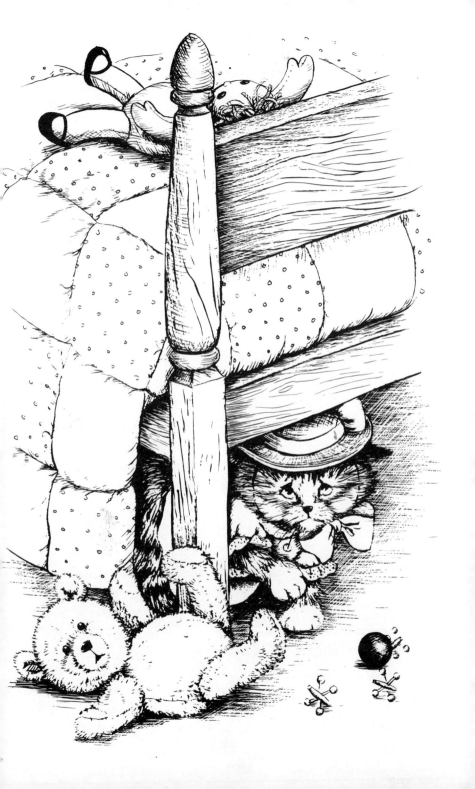

Sarah and I also had a game I didn't like. It was called "Dress the Cat."

I was the cat.

Sarah would take me to her room and close the door. Then she would take the clothes off one of her dolls and try to put them on me.

A hat would smush my ears down. A blouse would feel tight around my arms, and a dress would make my tummy hurt. I didn't like stuff like that on me. Clothes aren't made for cats.

Usually, I'd jump down and hide under the bed. Sometimes Sarah would find me and make me play the game again. Sometimes she would go off and do something else. I'd wait under the bed until I was sure she was gone, then march off down the hall, swishing my tail, just like Toby had taught me.

It was a disgusting game.

But the worst game was something I didn't even know was a game at first. It was a terrible game. The worst of all.

It was called "Snot Stew."

Chapter 9

Toby and I had lived with the Burkes about three weeks when Ben and Sarah first played Snot Stew. Ben and Sarah had just started off for a place called School.

Ben and Sarah fussed and griped and said they didn't want to go to school. So I figured school was a bad place. But the first morning, when they walked to the end of the road and a big yellow bus came to pick them up, Mother closed the front door and gave Daddy a big hug.

"Isn't school wonderful?" she said.

When Ben and Sarah got home, they talked and laughed about all the neat things that happened at school. But the next morning, when it was time to go again, they'd gripe and fuss.

So I couldn't tell whether school was a good place or a bad place.

Anyway, the house was really quiet with Ben and Sarah gone. When they came home in the afternoons, they were ready to play. Toby and Ben would play Chase the String or roughhouse with each other. My Sarah would sometimes play rough with me. Usually, we played People Scratch. She would sit down in front of the TV, and I would jump up in her lap, and she would scratch and pet me. I liked that.

After we played awhile, Ben and Sarah would have to do homework. They would lie down on the floor with their books and make scratchy marks on paper with their pencils.

Toby would lie in his chair, and I would curl up in my safe place, under the couch.

One evening while Ben and Sarah were doing their homework, Sarah picked up a pencil. Ben yanked it away from her.

"That's mine," he growled.

Sarah frowned.

"Is not."

Ben frowned back.

"Is too."

"Is not."

"Is too."

"Isnot!"

"Istoo!"

"Snot!"

"Stoo!"

My eyes flashed open. I stood up so fast my head hit the bottom of the couch.

STEW?

Did somebody say STEW?

I thought to myself, I LOVE STEW.

I raced out from under the couch and charged toward the kitchen. It had been such a long time since we'd had stew, I could hardly wait. Toby followed me.

But when we got to the kitchen, there was no stew. There was nothing in our bowls but that stuff they called Dry Cat Food.

My whiskers twitched from side to side.

"There's no stew."

Toby wiggled his whiskers, too.

"What kind of deal is this?" he meowed. "They said, 'stew.' And there's none here."

We waited in the kitchen for a while, thinking maybe Mother would bring our stew soon. Mother just kept reading her book.

Finally, feeling sad and disappointed, we went back to the living room.

"It's not fair," I pouted. "I love stew. They said stew and . . . and . . . there's not any."

Toby nodded.

"Yeah. Mama was right. You can't trust people things. That was really a mean trick."

The next night it happened again.

Mother was doing some knitting. I played with the end of the string until Mother finally started playing People Scratch. Toby crawled up in Daddy's lap. Daddy shoved him off, but Toby just crawled back again. Finally, Daddy decided to play People Scratch too.

Mother was busy with her knitting, but she would stop every now and then to scratch me. It felt good, just lying next to her. Mother was warm and soft.

Everything was quiet. Everything was comfortable and nice.

Then Sarah got a piece of gum and started to unwrap it.

"That's mine," Ben growled.

Sarah glared at him.

"Is not."

He glared back.

"Is too."

"Is not."

"Is too."

"Is not."

"Is too."

"Isnot!"

"Istoo!"

"Snot!"

"Stoo!"

I stood up so fast my head knocked Mother's ball of yarn off her lap. It rolled across the floor.

STEW! My eyes popped wide open. Oh boy, I thought. I LOVE STEW."

I raced for the kitchen.

All of a sudden, Daddy yelled, "Ouch!"

Toby had jumped off Daddy's lap and was racing after me.

But when we got to the kitchen, our bowls were empty. There wasn't even any dry cat food. Toby scooted up real close to me and looked back at the door.

"I think I'm in trouble," he whispered.

"Why?"

"When Ben and Sarah said 'stew,' I took off so fast I accidentally stuck one of my claws in Daddy's leg.

Mother and Daddy appeared at the door.

Daddy glared down at us. "Darned crazy cats," he growled. "What the devil's wrong with them?"

Mother picked her ball of yarn up from the floor.

"Beats me," she answered. "Maybe a mouse or something."

I shook my head. "No, it's the stew," I meowed. "Ben said there was stew, and we can't find it."

Only Mother and Daddy couldn't understand. They looked at us awhile, then shook their heads and went back to sit down.

Toby twitched his whiskers from side to side.

"There's something wrong here. Before, whenever somebody said 'stew,' there was stew. Now there's nothing. What's going on?"

I flipped my tail.

"Right before they say 'stew,' one says 'snot.' Maybe snot stew is different from regular stew."

The next night Sarah brought her doll with her when she lay on the floor with Ben to do homework. Her doll wasn't much help. It was so dumb it didn't even read her book, much less help her scratch on the paper with her pencil.

From my safe place under the couch I watched Ben. Very slowly, he snuck his hand across the floor. Then he got hold of Sarah's doll's arm and started scooting it back toward him.

But Sarah caught him.

"That's mine!"

Ben pulled the doll's arm.

"Is not."

Sarah stuck out her bottom lip.

"Is too."

"Is not."

"Is too."

"Isnot!"

"Istoo!"

"Snot!"

"Stoo!"

Snot stew. I thought to myself. I'm not falling for that one again. Only, I couldn't help myself. I LOVE STEW. But this time, instead of running to the kitchen, Toby and I just walked.

Again—there was nothing in our bowls.

"I don't understand," I told Toby.

He looked back at Ben and Sarah. They were yanking the doll back and forth, yelling: "Snot! Stew!"

Toby smiled.

Daddy was reading the paper. He yanked it down, slapping it hard against his leg.

"You two shut up," he roared. "Either hush that or go to your rooms."

Toby's smile got even bigger.

"What is it, Toby?" I wondered. "Why are you smiling?"

"I think I got it figured out," he answered.

"What?"

"Snot stew. I think I know what it is."

I felt my eyes get real big. "Really? What is it?"

Toby smiled confidently.

"It's a game," he said. "A game like Pushie-Shove. I figured it out when they were pulling the doll back and forth. Only, instead of being called Pushie-Shove, it's called Snot Stew."

My nose crinkled up on one side.

"You know, Toby. I think you're right. It's not stew at all. It's just another dumb game."

Toby strolled back toward his chair.

"I don't know whether it's so dumb or not. Ben and Sarah seem to have fun playing it. They play it enough; they *must* like it."

Frowning, I followed him.

"I don't know, Toby. It's a loud game. They always act mad and mean when they play."

Toby flipped his tail.

"It looks like fun to me," he meowed. "Tomorrow let's play Snot Stew."

I didn't really want to play. But Toby's my brother, and if he thought it would be fun . . .

Chapter 10

The next morning I'd almost forgotten about Snot Stew. Mother let us outside early. Toby played chase with Butch a few times. I rolled in the dirt and lay in the sun. After a little while Mother opened the door.

"Here kitty, kitty, kitty," she called in a real high voice. "You two ready to eat?"

We only had dry cat food, but being outside always made me hungry. I started to eat.

All of a sudden, Toby bopped me over the ears with his paw.

"Mine," he meowed.

I frowned at him.

"No it's not. This is my bowl."

Toby made a mean face.

"It is not."

I glared back at him.

"It is too."

He arched his back.

"Is not."

"Is too."

"Is not."

"Istoo."

"Snot!"

"Stoo!"

Then he jumped at me. He grabbed me around the ears with his front paws and pretended to kick me in the stomach with his back ones. We rolled and tumbled on the floor, playfully biting and chewing at each other.

"We're playing Snot Stew," Toby growled.

And we laughed and laughed.

After we finished eating, I curled up under the couch to give myself a cat bath. Maybe Snot Stew isn't such a bad game after all, I thought. Toby and I haven't wrestled and played so much since we were kittens. Maybe Snot Stew is a good thing.

But too much of even a good thing can cause problems.

It seemed like Toby wanted to play Snot Stew all the time. And it seemed like the more we played, the rougher Toby got. One day when we were eating, he even hit me with his claws, instead of just boxing me with his paw.

That hurt!

"I don't want to play Snot Stew anymore," I complained, licking where Toby scratched me. "Let's quit."

Toby just walked over to my bowl and shoved me out of the way.

"If you don't want to play—fine! I'll just eat your food, too. Then it *will* be mine."

I sat there, smoothing my fur with my tongue. Toby gobbled my food up, then went back to his own bowl.

The same thing happened the next day and the next.

After a week I could almost feel my ribs sticking out. I hated Snot Stew. It was the dumbest, stingiest, most selfish game I'd ever played. It was no fun at all.

After a second week of Snot Stew my brother Toby was a different cat. He was grouchy all the time. He was lazy, too. He didn't want to play or even climb trees. All he wanted to do was lie around and sleep. I think he really liked bossing me and taking my food.

It wasn't a game for him. Not anymore. Snot Stew was real. Toby wanted everything of mine. He wanted to play with my Sarah after she got home from school. He wanted to eat my food. He even tried to take over my safe place under the couch. Only, Toby had gotten a lot bigger and fatter from eating both my food and his. He had trouble squeezing under my couch.

At least I still have my safe place, I thought.

Around lunchtime I noticed a wonderful smell coming from the kitchen. I was hungry, and the smell kept drifting to my nose and making little drops of water form at the corners of my mouth.

I could hear the *tink* sound when Mother put the dishes on the table. Daddy came in, and when they finished eating, Mother opened the door.

"Rambo. Tic-tac," she called.

Those were our people names, so we didn't act like we heard her.

"Come on, you two," she coaxed. "If you're ready to eat, I've got some stew."

My eyes rolled in my head. My tongue lapped across my lips.

"I love stew," I swooned, jumping up to trot to the kitchen.

But Toby got there first. He was eating out of *my* bowl. He was eating *my* stew.

"Can I eat my stew?" I asked politely.

Toby just sneered at me and flipped his tail.

"It's not yours; it's mine."

I shoved him.

"It is not."

He shoved back.

"Is too."

I'll show you, I thought. I'll just eat your stew.

But when I got to Toby's bowl, he waddled over and shoved me aside.

"This is mine, too," he growled.

"Is not," I growled back.

"Is too."

I felt my teeth grind together. I was *not* going to play Snot Stew.

I HAD HAD IT!

Before I knew what happened, I flew into him with everything I had. I jumped on his back and hung on with my claws. I hissed. Me-owed. Growled. Bit his ear. Chewed the back of his neck.

Toby didn't know what hit him at first. But he fought back. He was much bigger and heavier than me. Suddenly, he flung me off. Then he pounced on me.

Clawing and biting and hissing and spitting, we rolled across the floor. We bumped into Mother's

leg. She was jumping from one foot to the other, screaming at us to stop.

We didn't.

I had had as much of Toby as I could take. He wasn't going to eat *my* stew. I bit him again.

All of a sudden, something cold and very wet hit me. I was just about to chomp down on Toby's paw. Instead, I shivered with the cold, wet feel. I jumped up to shake myself off.

Mother stood, glaring down at us. She had an empty water glass in her hand.

Before either of us had time to dry ourselves with our paws or tongue, she snatched us up by the backs of our necks.

"I'll not have that fighting in my house," her voice boomed. "If you two are going to fight, you can do it outside."

And with that she flung us out the back door.

I was dripping wet. My tail was even wet. I guess that's what threw my balance off. I managed to land on my feet, but instead of staying on them, I fell over and went rolling.

Now the water Mother had poured on us was *mud*.

Toby managed to stay on is feet, but his tummy was so round and full of *my* stew that it bounced against the ground. I heard him make kind of a "whoosh" sound. It knocked the air out of him. He stood there a minute, trying to catch his breath.

I was so mad at Toby I didn't even want to talk to him. I marched over and sat under the tree. I started licking my paws, then rubbing my fur, to try to get the nasty, yucky mud off me.

Once Toby caught his breath, he acted like he couldn't care less that we'd been thrown out of the house. He flipped his tail—real smart-alec-like— and headed for the picnic table.

"Haven't given ole Butch a run for quite a while," he said, wiggling his ears. "Think we'll play chase."

The dirt that was now mud stuck to my paws. I got some of it in my mouth. I used my tongue, trying to get the gritty feel out from beneath my teeth.

"Hope he gets you," I spit.

Toby ignored me. He jumped up on the picnic table, then to the fence rail. Like always, he pranced down the rail to his usual spot. He looked around until he found Butch.

"Hey, Fatty," he meowed. "Bet you can't catch me. Fatty, fatty, two-by-four . . ."

Then he jumped down.

I heard Butch bark. Outside the fence, I could hear him chasing Toby. I could hear him growling and roaring. I could hear his teeth snapping together.

I yawned.

Then, just as usual, Toby appeared at the hole in the fence.

Just as usual, his head came through the hole. And just as usual, his front paws came through. Then—*not as usual*—Toby stopped. I quit licking my fur and sat up.

Suddenly, his eyes got as big around as saucers. He lunged. Jerked.

Nothing happened. Toby didn't move.

Outside the fence, I could hear Butch roar. He was getting closer.

"I'm stuck," Toby meowed. "Help me! I'm stuck in the hole!"

Butch's bark was a roar. Toby's eyes flashed open even wider than before. His ears shot straight up. He jerked one more time, but it was no use.

"OOOOUUCH!" Toby screamed. "MEOOOO-OOOWWWW! That hurts."

His eyes were filled with panic. He clawed the ground.

"He's got me! Butch is eating me!"

Toby's cry was the most frantic, most terrible sound I'd ever heard in my life.

Chapter 11

Before I even knew what was happening, I was on my feet. Every muscle in my body was tense. My ears were flat against my neck.

I charged across the yard and leaped to the picnic table, then to the fence rail. Not once did I even think about falling off as I raced forward.

I stopped above Toby. He was clawing the ground. Screaming. Crying.

I climbed to the top of the fence and looked down.

Butch was there, right behind Toby. He was snarling and growling and chomping.

He was eating my brother's tail!

Behind me, I heard the back door slam. I heard Mother's voice say: "What in the world? What's all this racket? Oh my gracious . . . !"

Butch had chomped his way almost to Toby's rear end.

I jumped!

All four legs were out straight. Each claw in each paw stuck out as far as I could make it. My tail spun, helping me keep my balance.

I hope I'm aiming right, I thought. Then I closed my eyes because I couldn't bear to watch.

I felt my long, sharp claws dig into something. My eyes flashed open. My aim had been good. I landed right where I wanted to, right square on Butch's back. My front claws dug into his floppy, black ears. My back claws hung tight to his back.

Butch stopped chomping on Toby.

I could feel his muscles tense beneath my claws. I dug them in deeper. Butch leaped up. I dug my claws in deeper.

"Yipe!" Butch barked.

Then we took off.

Butch yiped and howled and squealed as we raced around the yard. He bounced up and down.

I hung on tighter.

He howled and shook himself all over.

I hung on even tighter.

He twisted and turned, but he couldn't reach me.

I just hung on.

Then I saw Toby's rear end disappear through the

hole in the fence. Butch lay down and started to roll over on me. I dug my claws in, hard as I could. And at the very last second . . . I let go. I raced as fast as I could for the hole under the fence.

Butch didn't chase me, although I didn't know that until I was on the other side of the fence. Only then did I stop and turn around to look.

Through the crack I could see him. The big black monster was still rolling on the ground. He would flip from side to side in the dirt—still trying to rub off the places where my claws had dug in.

Mother was carrying Toby through the back door.

I raced after them, but I was too late. She disappeared inside the house yelling for Daddy.

I was panting. My heart was pounding so hard it felt like it was going to come out of my throat.

"Let me in," I meowed. "I want to see Toby. Is he still alive? Let me in."

Inside, I could hear her yelling: "James. James. Help me. No. I've got a towel. Go check on Tic-tac."

Daddy came racing to the door. He flung the door open, and I trotted in to see what had happened to Toby.

"She's all right," James called from behind me. I guess James was Daddy's other name. I'm not sure because most of the time Mother called him Daddy.

"What happened?" Daddy James wanted to know.

Mother cupped a dish towel under Toby's hind end.

"That dumb dog of yours caught Rambo. He would have killed him if Tic-tac hadn't jumped on his back and startled him." Mother looked down at me, then at Daddy James. "She's always been such a 'fraidy-cat. So timid and shy and mild-mannered. I couldn't believe she attacked that dog of yours."

"My dog," Daddy James yelped. "I'll have you know, Pat, that dog is as much yours as mine. You helped pick him out, remember. You . . ."

"Oh, hush," Mother Pat told Daddy James. "Rambo's bleeding all over my dish towel and my floor. We better get him to the vet's."

I tried to follow them. I called to Toby, but he wouldn't answer me. He kept meowing—stuff about his tail and how he hurt. At the front door, when I tried to go with them, Daddy James shoved me back with his foot.

"I want to go," I meowed.

He shut the door.

I was so worried about Toby. Would he be all right? Would I ever see him again? I kept pacing back and forth in front of the door.

"Meow. Meow." I called his name over and over.

I heard the car start. Then the sound moved farther and farther away, down the road.

I was so scared, so worried. I couldn't even crawl under the couch and rest in my safe place. All I could do was pace back and forth across the living room. Finally, I crawled up to the window. I sat on the window sill and watched the road. I prayed that they would bring Toby back.

At long, long last my prayers were answered.

Mother and Daddy drove up in their car, just before the yellow school bus brought Ben and Sarah home.

They carried Toby inside and laid him down in his chair. Mother brought towels and put them under him. Ben and Sarah came in, but Mother and Daddy wouldn't let them mess with Toby. They made them go in the kitchen to do their homework. They said Toby needed his rest.

Finally, after Ben and Sarah and Mother and Daddy went into the other room, I jumped down from the window sill. I went to Toby's chair.

Toby was almost asleep. He could barely hold his eyes open.

"Are you okay?" I meowed.

Toby tried to smile.

"I think so." He propped himself up on one paw.

"They gave me a shot to make me rest. I'm sure sleepy."

"How bad is it?" I asked.

Toby flopped his head toward his tail.

"Not too bad. They sewed my tail up. Wrapped it in white stuff called gauze and put sticky stuff called tape on it. But . . . but . . . but . . ."

Toby stopped and sniffed back a tear.

"But what?" I urged.

"But my tail's gone. Butch ate my tail."

I jumped up, gently, to sit in the chair beside him.

"Here," I said. "Lay your head on my paws."

Toby lay down and closed his eyes.

"I'm sorry," I whispered. "It's all my fault. It's all my fault."

Toby sat up. His sleepy eyes didn't seem sleepy anymore.

"Your fault?" he growled. "What makes you think that? If it hadn't been for you, Butch would have eaten me."

I shook my head.

"No. It's all my fault. If I hadn't gotten in a fight with you over the stew. If I hadn't said 'I hope he gets you.' If . . ."

Toby licked my ears.

"Oh, hush that. It wasn't your fault. It's me. If I

hadn't been so busy playing Snot Stew and eating all your food, then I wouldn't have gotten so fat that I couldn't squeeze through the hole in the fence. Butch would have never gotten me if I hadn't got stuck.

"You saved me. I never knew you were so brave. If you hadn't jumped on his back . . . You know, you risked your life to save me. You're the bravest sister in the whole wide world."

He licked my ears a few more times; then his sleepy head went *kerplop* on my paws.

In the other room, I could hear Ben and Sarah.

"That's my pencil," Ben snapped.

"Is not," Sarah griped back.

"Is too."

"Is not."

"Is too."

"Isnot!"

"Istoo!"

"Snot!"

"Stoo!"

Toby rolled over. He raised his wobbly head and licked my cheek.

"I'll never play Snot Stew again," he told me.

*   *   *

Toby was up and around in no time. He was a different cat after his experience with Butch. Toby was nice and easy to get along with. We shared our food. We shared our Ben and our Sarah. We shared everything.

Toby didn't tease the big dog anymore. He hardly ever got smart-alec with me, and he never pranced around and flipped his tail.

Of course, he didn't have a tail to flip. All he had was a stub.

And we never, ever played Snot Stew again.